Glaze

Mimie

Ukiyoto Publishing

All global publishing rights are held by

Ukiyoto Publishing

Published in 2022

Content Copyright © Mimie

ISBN 9789362696250

All rights reserved.

No part of this publication may be reproduced, transmitted, or stored in a retrieval system, in any form by any means, electronic, mechanical, photocopying, recording or otherwise, without the prior permission of the publisher.

The moral rights of the author have been asserted.

This is a work of fiction. Names, characters, businesses, places, events, locales, and incidents are either the products of the author's imagination or used in a fictitious manner. Any resemblance to actual persons, living or dead, or actual events is purely coincidental.

This book is sold subject to the condition that it shall not by way of trade or otherwise, be lent, resold, hired out or otherwise circulated, without the publisher's prior consent, in any form of binding or cover other than that in which it is published.

www.ukiyoto.com

To those who believed in me, you know who you are.

CONTENTS

Passive Voice	1
How to Time Travel	6
Home Invader	12
Summon Help!	18
About the Author	*23*

Passive Voice

Taylor woke up startled. She did not know if she dreamt that she heard something weird and woke up, or she woke up because she heard something weird for real. "What the f-" she muttered under her breath. She looked around her room, scampering like a wild animal, with the foot of her lampshade in hand. Cautiously examining every corner of her minimalist white bedroom, Her heartbeat raised a bit, but she tried to think rationally. Seeing that nothing was actually amiss, she filled up her tub with warm water, and dropped in a lavender-chamomile bath bomb. It's a little unusual without the darkness and her tealights, but it'll have to do. Her hands, visibly shaking, stirred up the water before she went in. She reached over and shuffled through the small wicker basket that housed some small towels, some essential oils, and her phone. I won't be able to come in in the morning, something's come up. I'll try to attend the 1pm. Sorry about this. She texted the office secretary, Geoff. She dipped her head in the water. For a few seconds, she soaked in the calm and silence. Not long after, her muted screams burbled up from beneath the sparkly, supposedly soothing water. Coffee. I probably just need coffee. She hurried and changed her clothes, took a thick hoodie and started off to the door. "SHUT UP!" She yelled.

Luckily, she had some music to distract her thoughts as she briskly walked to the coffee shop nearby. She played some old Linkin Park tunes she grew up with in High School. This used to give her a sense of comfort and nostalgia, but now it just serves as a loud distraction, which only seems to be making things worse. She took off her earpods and stuffed them in her jeans. She tried to calm herself as she noticed that her breathing was going faster than usual, even before coffee. Coffee calms me down. She thought, even if she knew scientifically about the effects of caffeine, and didn't really know if she believes it. "Shut up! Shut up! Shut up!" She muttered under her breath.

Taylor was now unsure why she cancelled her morning office work. She knew she needed some sorting out to do right now inside of her head, but she didn't exactly know how that's going to happen, where she'd go, and how to go about it. It seems like she could've been better off distracting herself with her office work than dealing with her chaotic mind. She wandered off, coffee in hand, and tried to find the best place to go and be alone on a Tuesday morning which didn't exactly present to be hard at all, if you think that most people in that saturated, downtown area should be mostly at work. But with her mind in a frenzy and her sense of stability threatening to dismantle, everywhere seemed to be teeming with life, and for once, in this instance, she detested that. Then she remembered the old movie theater that closed down long ago where students were allowed to practice in after a cult got kicked out of it when the owner found out they made it their home-base for about a decade. It wasn't being used all the time, the students very rarely practice there because they think the place is kind of haunted, and she could make all the noise she wants without a soul getting suspicious! How she managed to jog while finishing most of her venti cup as she arrived was a mystery for another day. Right now, she had to deal with whatever it was that's consistently chattering inside her head.

"WHO THE HELL ARE YOU?! WHAT DO YOU WANT?!? PLEASE JUST GO AWAY!" She screamed desperately. She looked around, knowing that she won't find anyone else in that stage, trying her utmost best to find the source of all her anxiety. She screamed out of frustration, out of desperation, and out of self pity—that her once "sane" and capable self is slowly fading away. What the hell is this? What did I do to deserve this? Why is this happening to me? What am I supposed to do? How can I get over this? Is this ever gonna go away? So many thoughts ran through her broken mind as Taylor tried to compose herself after her little break down. She wiped away her tears and snot with her sleeve, and thanked fate that she didn't put on any make-up yet. But it was almost noon, and she had to pull herself together and get ready for work. She almost enjoyed being alone in the theater, now that she thought of having to go to work in her state, but she also remembered Jeanna. *Jeanna can help me.* She thought.

So she went back home, changed into her most "I mean business" business suit, put on make-up that would mask all her innermost anxieties, and headed to her 1pm meeting. Good thing this was one of those that could actually be sufficiently emailed that everyone would groan about later when it's all over, and she wasn't required to present anything. Her mind looped a single message throughout the whole hour, which was "Must talk to Jeanna." She understood none of it. She found Jeanna at Geoff's table at the entrance. She's usually there flirting, unknowingly, to an openly gay man, and she's in therapy for it. Well, for "relationship problems". But mainly, it's for somehow being weirdly attracted to mostly gay men. She had a three-year relationship to one who found out that HE was gay after dating her and finding out her weird inclination towards them. After that whole ordeal, she got into occult stuff, and got into tarot reading, crystals, candles, demonology and the like. She started out wanting to hex the poor, unwittingly closeted guy, but didn't go through with it after she found out that it might come back to her three times as powerful if he was 'protected' or have consulted other witches. Eventually, her interest just grew naturally. Maybe she'd have some input with the voices she hears in her head. Taylor wasn't normally into that heeby-jeeby stuff, but she's desperate to know just what is going on.

"Jeanna," she called. "Jeanna, can I have some more of that oil for a bit?" Taylor has previously bought a little vial of blue lotus oil for her bath bombs once from Jeanna. She loved the smell of that oil, but didn't know it had some pretty soporific and mildly intoxicating effects as well, when used in a different way. "Oh honey, let's have a chat in the girls' room shall we? I do need a little touch-up."

Jeanna took Taylor's arm and whisked her to the ladies room, and popped out her vial bag. They were completely organized like a tiny, portable apothecary in a floral wrap of canvas and leather. "You took a hit, didn't you?" She smiled slyly. "Actually, I just need more for my bath bombs, but that's not exactly why I wanted to talk to you..." Taylor opened up to Jeanna and told everything that happened that morning, including her little theatrical break down just a couple of hours prior. Jeanna was just the perfect weirdo to open up to because she seemed to have much weirder experiences, and especially since they were both kind of walking the line on some crazy substances and realities. She took out some disproportionately huge cards and shuffled them around until a couple stuck out and got caught by its corner. La Luna. El Ahorcado. She took out her inverted pyramid, rose-quartz necklace and held it up like some sort of offering to the gods or something, and it shook every which way as Jeanna spoke stuff in Spanish. "This is some interdimensional shit you're going through, and is pretty much outside of my capabilities... but what my spirit guides are saying to me is that you should just let it happen and move on with your life, however that can be possible. I know I might get just as exasperated as you if not more, so..." she shuffled and took out a card from her huge vintage bag, "... maybe she can help."

'Dr. Jodi Forresten PhD., PsyD., L.P.C.C.' Read the card. At this point, Taylor didn't care that even Jeanna, of all people, thinks that she's proper crazy. What the hell, I've been going through this for a single day, and I've lost my bearings, how many times now? I just want this THING out of my head as soon as possible! She took the card, dialed it in and called. She set up an appointment that very week, telling her secretary that she needs to be seen as soon as possible, and that it was an emergency. "Are you having thoughts right now of hurting yourself or committing suicide?" Asked the unnervingly cool voice behind the phone. "Oh, I just might. I have no idea what I'm capable of, and it kind of scares me!" There was a brief pause. Taylor had no idea why she said what she said, as she's normally just your average girl who wants no trouble, and tries to blend in and not attract attention. Well, she might not be normal anymore, but that's definitely what she feels. "SHUT THE HELL UP!" Even Jeanna was shocked at the outburst. She lit some sage and started smudging and chanting affirmations in the ladies room for the both of them.

The appointment was set later that evening at 6:30pm. Her card had a printed schedule on it that said M-W-F, 9:00am—5:00pm. Not only was she not on schedule, she was not even on the time slot. She was almost sorry Dr. Forresten went out of her way to schedule her right then, but she wasn't. She wanted her life back. This, after spending a day with the voices in her head. She just can't take it.

"So... What brings you here?" Jodi asked. "It started this morning, and it won't stop! These voices are making me crazy!..." Taylor was shaking. "What kind of voices? Can you describe them? What do they say?" "They're different all the time. I can't make out if they're men or women... I'm scared," Taylor was tearing up. "What do they tell you?" Jodi prodded. Taylor looked straight at her, wide-eyed, "... Taylor was tearing up. What do they tell you? Jodi prodded..."

How to Time Travel

If some scientist happens to pick up this manual and actually make use of any information laid out by my first-hand experience on time travel, that would be so awesome. I can't write those things myself as I am just a regular guy who is kind of obsessed about this girl, who happened to lose my grip on my supposed reality, my then "present". By doing so, I have seen the expanse of what time is like, and I will try to the best of my capacity to explain what I have perceived.

Space and time are not two sides of the same coin in my experience. I've read about bending space to make wormholes and stuff but that is just barely touching the whole idea of what time is. Time is so much bigger than that. Now, I am not an expert on space, but I do think that space is much harder to move through, it being made up of matter and all. I can't really talk too much about space as I only went through time. If there are other time travellers out there, you'd know what I'm talking about. I mean, I couldn't be the only one who gets to observe it out of billions of people, right?

1. Time is a coordinate

People tend to misunderstand the concept of time. We are all taught as children how to tell time with clocks, timelines, time tables and all these charts and graphs that demonstrate time in a linear and non-reversing, indefinite, continued progress of existence. I can assure you that it is not, and it is more complicated than that.

Time, in my experience, is more of a coordinate. It is a direction in which you tell in which area you are at, much like north, south, east and west, except you include other dimensions as well. You can move through time in infinite ways, and I learned this the hard way.

Like everyone else, I thought we moved in a single line forward through time, and maybe we could have the possibility to move backward in the future, like in the movies. What I didn't know is that there are infinite "forwards" we could choose from, and we only choose a single possibility. If you could imagine a tree, the roots would be the instances that lead us to our path. The trunk would be the past we chose, leading to the present, which would be the point before it splits into branches and leaves - the futures. There are an infinite number of futures, some similar and some absurdly different from each other. What future you land on will highly depend on what choices you make in the present. This is an oversimplification of course, which you will understand as you read along on my journey.

I did it by accident at first. I was on my way to see the new girl I was dating, then I found myself a bit confused and disoriented by the subtle but abrupt change in scenery. What was a lazy stroll in the outskirts of the city during sunset, turned into a bright noon time in the same area, but with new buildings and a lot of flying drones carrying differently sized packages. I wasn't sure what was happening so in my initial surprise I just figured I might've just been seeing things and kind of forgot about what I was doing. It took about 20 minutes of conscious effort so I could make sure I was in the right place, of just thinking about what I was supposed to be doing, when it was, and how I got there before I found myself somehow on the same sunset route to Jiemi's place.

2. Hills and Dips

While travelling through time regularly, you will notice that in the space scape you're travelling there will face many hills and dips, much like when hiking. Travelling towards the future tends to be easier, much like going down a hill, compared to travelling back to the past which resembles climbing up.

It's really a weird feeling, and the first accidental trip really encapsulates the sensation of sliding down or falling. I do think travelling to the past can happen if you intentionally go for it for your first trip, but it won't be easy, and it will probably never happen unintentionally. Furthermore, it will be extremely exhausting.

When I landed on my first future trip, it took a while to get my bearings and think straight. My first thought was "What's going on?", which isn't a very useful thought in hindsight, but probably unavoidable in my circumstance. It would have been better to think "When am I?", but I only learned that from experience. It didn't help that when I got to Jiemi's, it was when she hated me enough to want to kill me.

She was never sure of herself and just a little bit neurotic when I was hanging out with her, which made me want to be with her and protect her even more, so this version of Jiemi (which I didn't know at the time was a future one) confused and hurt me more than what she tried to do physically. The Jiemi I knew and loved was a bit shy, and a bit anxious about many things, but never really aggressive. She got nervous riding the subway alone so I had to be with her if she wanted to go somewhere far. In hindsight, it was pretty understandable when she got confused and emotional when I somehow got back from that first trip. I mean, I was too, but neither of us had any idea of what was happening at the time, and I was wrong for lashing out when she visited me by surprise at my apartment the moment I got back. I didn't know I was back, but I still regret that moment ever since, and am still trying to get myself to avoid it.

But, my 7m I digress. Going back to the "present" was something I figured out that I should do consciously and intentionally from my experience, as I only was able to do so after 2 weeks of her and her hired hands chasing me all over the city. I missed the Jiemi that I knew and I thought of her, and all the things that I knew of my life before it became this haywire crap of a situation, until I turned up at a familiar place. The only problem in this was, I didn't know that this familiarity meant that I came back to my respective time. This has caused me a lot more trouble than when I first travelled in the future, so I implore you, always ask yourself; "When am I?" whether or not you have the intention to travel across time. This brings us to the next rule, which is:

3. Always confirm your location

As I have mentioned before, time is not a linear thing. It just so happens that most of us, unaware of time's true nature, have been acting like pebbles tumbling down a narrow facet of time's vastness - When in fact time can be more akin to an ocean. And each time you swim to a different part of it, you send ripples and bubbles everywhere, which in turn affects the whole area you've been travelling on and changes the whole environment. This is why it is important to know that you cannot travel to the exact location twice. Travelling once has already disturbed the past where you came from, and going 'back' is not necessarily going to be the same past you've experienced. The knowledge you've gained through your trip has already changed the time from which you came.

Hence, it is essential to always check the date and time you have arrived by any means necessary. It was understandable when I first experienced the differences because they were very subtle. One moment I was just happily walking along the narrow cement block alley to Jiemi's, the next I was being pursued by men in black with matching masks, hats and shades. I hurriedly stumbled my way to Jiemi's to see if she was okay, only to discover her raging and being the person who ordered the hit. I didn't know why she was so mad, we've only been dating for a couple of weeks, and I'm totally into her, but this was unprecedented, at least to me. I mean, how was I to know that it was the future at the time? I haven't even been the person she hated yet! But I guess this was the start of it all.

4. The "present" does not exist (you are never in the same place twice)

Because you are never in the same time twice, this means the pasts and the futures you have travelled to virtually no longer exist. Theoretically, it still exists there in the sea of time, but finding it is like looking for a single specific plankton in the Pacific ocean. And if you do find it, you have to assemble all it's cells scattered about everywhere else. So there's really no such thing as a true 'present' except for when and where you currently are.

At the moment I am still in the process of trying to find the timeline when I never travelled. I don't even know if I will ever find it, having already done it myself. It will be a difficult ordeal, since it will involve travelling the 'incline' of the past and looking for a specific timeline that I am not even sure if it exists.

So far I have gone through multiple futures and pasts that all don't feel quite right, and mostly just ending up with Jiemi trying to kill me or loathe me at the very least. She didn't take my current situation that great. I didn't mean to travel at first, and it really messed her up when I returned multiple times as different versions of myself, having experienced many different futures each time I saw her. I can't really blame her, I was such a mess during those first few jumps. At first I was so scared of her I literally ran from her. The next couple of times I came back really angry and desperate to know why she was pursuing me and trying to murder me, when she didn't even do anything and was actually trying to surprise me by visiting unexpectedly. Some of the times I came back injured and blaming her, others I was crying and depressed, trying to woo her back. Of course in hindsight, it seemed as if I was going insane. Maybe I was. But I've resolved to find that time when I never did all these things. I may have experienced - and will probably continue to experience - loss and hardships concerning Jiemi. It's nothing new anymore, and I will endure them. After all, I have all the time in the world.

5. Everything is arbitrary

It's really difficult to compare time to anything, really. Trees, hills, and oceans can't even describe the qualities that time possesses in a manner where it can be fully known by a person who only experiences it in the typical, linear fashion. I can only make analogies and it seems quite nonsensical to describe time like all of them are even remotely alike, let alone the same thing. But like trees, it branches out. Like hills, the effort it takes to travel is more exhausting in one way than another.

Like an ocean, it changes with every wave. Like reaching for bubbles, the more you try to get to them, the more they fly away. Like a chinese finger trap, the more you want to escape it, the more it clings to you. The more rules you discover, the more you realize that there are a lot of exceptions to the rules. The more you understand, the more it gets complicated. So to keep everything simple, it's so much easier to imply that everything is just arbitrary.

But if I did encapsulate how I have experienced time in its entirety, I guess I would liken it to a snow globe. Space would be what's shown inside, and time is the water containing everything. Normally, we'd be the little speckles of snowflakes landing after it had been shook for a while, landing on the bottom in one straight path. I would just so happen to have my globe shook again and again by constantly traveling. But who knows, I just might land in my intended spot in the end.

Home Invader

Melinda woke with a start. It was 12am on her clock, and she had heard a crash right outside the bedroom. She was shivering from both the early morning, misty air coming through the half-open windowpanes of the bedroom she used to share with her late husband Tomas, and also from the blood-pumping fear she has of home-invaders. She lives alone for goodness' sake! How would a feeble, solitary woman protect herself in such cases? She tiptoed towards the door and arms herself with the coat hanger that used to be attached on the door, which eventually gave way. Now that her husband's gone, the broken things in her house stay broken until her son and/or daughter comes to either fix or buy her new things. Anyway, it's better than nothing. She could scare a man more with a coat hanger than with nothing, she believed.

She went down the narrow hallway that adjoins all the other rooms. None of the family pictures were disturbed, so the culprit might not have gotten to the rooms yet. It was quite the irony to feel so scared whilst surrounded by the faces of the people you loved. The fact remained that she was alone, and she was, sooner or later, going to face this threat.

The carpet under her feet muffled her steps, but the old wooden floors gave a small grunt when her foot left the floor. She felt as if that slightest sound might alarm whoever it is trespassing, of her presence, and might get her into danger. She peeked at the corner towards the living room. A shadowy figure of a spiky haired man was standing, holding a picture frame. Suddenly, she felt a hand land on her shoulder and gasped in alarm. "Mom?" Melinda turned and saw her daughter's lovely face painted in confusion. "Annie!" she sighed exasperatingly. "I thought you were a burglar! Here I was with a 'weapon' and all. Who's that guy in the living room?" Malinda asked, "And what are you doing here in the middle of the night?" "What guy? I came here alone this time, and it's 8 in the morning mom. Tommie's going to be late. And that's a coat hanger mom, not exactly weapon material." She mused. "But there was a guy in the living room!" Melinda argued. "He was holding my wedding photo on the table just a while ago!" "Maybe you just mistook Jing. Look, there she is with juice for us. Come!"

Melinda was confused, but was happy that she was wrong. Maybe her clock's batteries were just waning, and with her room on the west, she couldn't have seen or felt the sunrise. It was a dewy morning after all. Plus, Jing's plastic headband stuck on her head in such a way that little wisps of deviant hair sprung out in every which way. Jing's an efficient house help, she thought, but her lack of aesthetic sense gives away her naiveté. Melinda chuckled as she sipped some orange juice with her daughter. "So, Tommie's coming? I do need him to fix that coat hanger." "Yup, He'll be with Brenda too. She just went for a check-up." Annie explained. "I can't believe she's 23 weeks in! I wonder what you're going to have, mama, a granddaughter or a mini Tommie?" she giggled "It doesn't matter," Melinda started. "I remember when I was pregnant with you, and Tommie was anxious. He said he wanted a little bro that'll go everywhere with him, and have wrestling matches and bike races with, and he was almost disappointed that you turned out to be a girl..." "Well, he's got no choice anyway! I turned out to be a lovely little girl didn't I?" Annie pouted, batting her eyelashes. "I thought I did!" her mother jokingly replied, "It didn't matter that you were a girl anymore, because you still had fierce wrestling matches and bike races, didn't you? You were the little brother Tommie was hoping for!" She said, showing her a picture of her and Tommie taken from far away by their dad, biking along the empty streets of their village. They used to be the only house on that street in Greenfields, and their nearest neighbor was three blocks away. Now the streets seemed narrower with all the cars parked in front of the houses almost attached to each other, and the only green you could see were the old trees.

"What was I hoping for?" a voice echoed across the room. Tom was always a loud guy. It's almost ironic how his wife Brenda had a really soft, almost cooing voice. "Mama was hoping you could fix this coat hanger already!" Annie hollered. Brenda waved from behind Tom "Hi!" she squeaked. Melinda looked at the side table at her right, where a lamp sat together with Tom and Brenda's wedding photo. "It was just like yesterday when I changed your diapers, and now you're going to have a child of your own!" she exclaimed, eyeing Brenda's small baby bump. "You and papa used to say that all the time after our wedding, diapers aren't a good image to ponder on a special day mom!" Tom replied as he scratched his head. Annie and Brenda laughed, and Melinda smiled uneasily. Tomas' voice rang in her head at Tommie's mention of 'Papa', but as Melinda tried to envision him at his wedding, he always seemed so far away, that she couldn't see his face.

Melinda was out the next day gardening outside, near the picket fence she always loved. It was a hobby of hers to craft Bonsai, which she learned from her grandfather. It was a relaxing hobby, pruning leaves, making room for new branches, creating roots for new plants... and it gave her a rewarding feeling of nurturing new life and controlling their growth. Now that Annie's in University and Tom has started a family, it feels nice to still be able to take care of things at home. She reached for her garden shears while she inspected the branches of the new plant she's nurturing, but it landed on a gloved hand of a stranger. He had sombre brown eyes and black spiky hair, which shone like lacquered piano keys under the sunlight. He handed her the shears, and smiled a sort of sad smile and was about to turn away, when Melinda said "Thank you." The stranger's eyes lit up a bit like a surprised child, and then bowed respectfully to her before turning away. Melinda noticed him holding a book. No, it's a brown photo album, much like the one where she placed Tom's baby pictures.

A crack of lightning scared the wits out of her before she noticed that it was raining hard. Jing was grabbing the back of her shirt and yelling "Maam! Maam!" as loudly as she possibly can, while holding her arm up like a shield against the torrents of wind and water slapping her face. They ran onto the porch and wrung their clothes. Jing had initially brought an umbrella with her, but it got mangled by the violent gusts that befell them. "I'll bring you a towel and fresh clothes ma'am," Jing initiated as she coiled her long hair and tried to wring it dry as well. "What were you doing for so long standing in the garden?" she asked. Melinda still held the shears. "I was just pruning the banaba... I didn't realize that it's late. What time is it?" "It's already 2pm ma'am, and your lunch is still waiting in the dining room." Jing stated. She ran inside the house and brought a fresh towel and a change of clothes. "Go take a warm shower first ma'am, or you'll get sick! I'll heat your food up for you." She smiled. "What about you?" Melinda inquired. "Don't worry ma'am, back in my home, we used to play in the rain. I bet city folk don't do much of that" Jing laughed. Melinda smiled her uncertain smile. She certainly didn't remember playing in the rain. Where did she play? She put off her thought for now and went straight to the bathroom for a nice, warm shower.

Melinda got to see the brown-eyed man on most of the mornings she's pruning her plants. Sometimes he watched her snip off the stray branches that sprouted in the awkward areas of the dwarfed-up tree, coiling copper wire around its arms and forming it into a beautiful shape. She invited him inside the garden to show him the other plants, and told him stories that happened long ago. It's amazing how easy it is to fetch those stories whenever he's with this man, but always seems to have a hard time remembering which switch turned off the right light at home, or what remote did which. This is how it must feel to get old, She thought. He said his name was Hiro. He didn't say much, and mostly just smiled and nodded his head. He did ask about a keychain Melinda had in her pocket once. It was made of bread dough. She and her children once made small sculptures out of bread dough once, and the one she carried was a stick figure, with little curls. Annie said it was her. Hiro fiddled about it and looked at it like how a child looks at a new toy. Melinda thought that maybe she should bring out something to eat for her guest, and so called for Jing. She rang their doorbell so that Jing would hear from inside, and went into the tool shed for a while to get the spray bottle with fertilizer. When she went out though, Jing was already there but Riel was gone. "What is it ma'am?" asked Jing. She was already used to Melinda ringing the doorbell when she needed her outside. "Oh, um... can you spray this on the plants?" she asked, a bit confused. "My head hurts. I think I'm going to rest for a while."

Melinda was in a Japanese garden. She was in fact, in Japan with her grandfather. Ito, as he was called, bought his plants in this particular place. "You know Melinda, the first bonsais were used to be acquired from cliffs," he said, "they were stunted trees that rooted on the rocks, which never stood tall like their brothers. They could never grow, but that's how we small creatures can appreciate them" "But aren't the bonsais jealous of the other trees?" she asked. "They don't know they're small," Ito explained, "so they believe they are just as great as the other trees, and they are!"

She woke feeling much more tired as before she slept, so Melinda tried to go into the kitchen and make some afternoon tea. Jing was out on her day off, and today some other girl came in her place. She was much neater than Jing. Her hair was in a tight bun, and her clothes were neatly pressed. "Patty," she called, "please reheat the food you cooked. I want to eat now." "Ahh, um, right away ma'am... um, should I use the microwave or the stove?" She was indeed neater and more appealing to the eye than Jing, but Jing had an air of expertise with her job. "Use the microwave. Put it in the Tupperware container first, the one on the shelf." Melinda instructed. It was already 1:30pm when she woke up, and she's starving. Hiro came later that day, and Melinda invited him for tea inside the house. She wasn't in the mood to go gardening today, as she didn't feel quite as lively as before, so she instructed Patty to tend to the plants. "Are you going to take another souvenir?" she asked Hiro. "What do you mean?" Hiro's guilty eyes looked up to her, and he frowned. "Oh I know all about it. I just don't understand why you do it." Melinda said. Hiro just looked at the floor and sighed. "Today, I might take more than what I usually do." He announced. He fiddled with the picture frame of Melinda's biking children and stared at it for a while.

"I'm sorry." "I knew you were the burglar!" Melinda exclaimed. "Please don't take anything anymore. I don't really have anything of value..." she persuaded, but Hiro immediately replied, "They have a lot of value Melinda, more than the frames, more than the material, and that is precisely why I need them." he said. "I liked you, you know... you remind me of someone, but I can't remember who." Melinda tried to delay him and coerce her friend to stop. She loved his company, and didn't want him to leave her alone, but hated the fact that this guy was a thief. "I need to go now." He lifted a black sports bag, and began to shove a few trinkets inside them. He took the picture, a pressed flower on a frame, some wedding favors, an origami crane with a childish note written on it, and a sketch of herself tending to her plants. Melinda shed a tear. She felt a hand grab hers, and saw patty with her wet face and trembling lips intently looking at her. "This drama always gets me crying too!" she announced, while the television blared out another rerun of "Maria la del Barrio". I miss Jing, she thought. When she looked around, it was evening, and Hiro was gone. She stood up and looked at the clock behind her. 7pm? That doesn't sound right. It seemed like it wasn't even 30 minutes since she woke up. "Did you see the man who was just here?" she asked Patty. "I didn't see any one besides you ma'am" she answered, "and I thought you were sleeping, but I guess... I guess you were watching the show." She manages to choke out between sobs.

Melinda didn't see Hiro for a while, and she was both a little glad and a little sad about it. She went on gardening every morning, half expecting to see him again by the fence, and half dreading more things to come in his possession. She did find a few more things missing since their last encounter though, and this time they were much bigger things like the old VHS player in her room, the glass goblets she got as a wedding gift, and a whole stack of gardening magazines. This time, she told Tom and Annie about a burglar stealing things in her house. Tom grew concerned, and hired a former carpenter to check up on her from time to time and help her with the household. Annie thought she was just being paranoid and forgetful though, and tried to ease her mother's fear. "Mom," she said, "maybe you were just dreaming. You tend to sleep a lot recently, and sometimes Jing says she even finds you napping while holding a pair of shears in the garden!" she said. "Maybe." Melinda half assuredly agreed. After all, how could she account for the lost time she's been experiencing? But to be safe, Annie convinced Tom to hire Patty full-time as well, just so there are more eyes in that big house.

Summon Help!

I was a bit excited when after 66 long years, somebody had the guts to summon me again in that huge house that was once polished and gleaming from the chandeliers hanging above to the sheen of the oiled wood banisters and flooring. A group of teenagers high from some grass and too curious about some book one of them found in one of their attics had called me as a "proof of concept" that the occult was not "evil" and "very useful". Their souls were not the best, but I've had my fill so I'm not complaining. I didn't think that house would degrade so much in just 66 years, but I did have to get my bearings for a moment as I didn't recognize the same driveway those teens did their seance, nor the new human who summoned me. Why was he so tiny? How did he know the ancient Latin incantation? What did he want from me? Now he's chanting it. I'm already here though!

It's not as if I can even use his soul too. I'm not sure how this pure being even got to summon me in the first place, he had naught the intention nor the slightest will for sure. "Raffy? Oh hi, you must be the new babysitter. I didn't expect you to be a... guy. Doesn't matter. Thanks for picking up Raffy! Come in, I was out here a while ago but I needed to get him a bottle. I'll show you where everything is and if you have any questions you can call me. I just need to get a few stuff in the store..." I was a bit baffled by this female human. I wasn't even in my human form, and she thought my figure was of a "babysitter"? I was used to reactions of fear, of disgust, recoiling in panic and hate. A few might have summoned up their courage to speak to me, or be crazed enough to actually command their wishes. But nobody was this... nice? Is that what this is?

I just picked up the 2 year old to see how I can make use of him or get out of this absurd situation, and now I am the babysitter. I was intrigued though, so I went with it. He wouldn't be able to demand a wish, and I can't really tarnish his pure soul, so I cannot take it either way. But his mom is interesting. I carried him inside in my most grotesque form, so one of the neighbors who happened to look fell from her bar stool while having breakfast. This confirmed that I was definitely not in my human disguise. "Make yourself at home Jasper, fridge is stocked except for some peanut butter, jelly and fruit snacks, which I'm gonna get, and if there's anything else, you can call me at this number." She hands me a little note. Her writing was terrible. She proceeded to make her way out and drove off. The toddler was still chanting, "Ego te voco Dagon Dagon Daaaagonnnn..." and proceeded to blow raspberries, which wasn't actually part of the summoning ritual, but was inconsequential. The marks on the driveway drawn by the teens of yesteryear were burnt in the driveway's brick path, but were actually covered up with a thin layer of cement. I don't know how that still worked, but here I am, Dagon, the wish-granter. But I thought I'd go by Jasper a little longer.

"Ding dong" I placed the babbling babe in a little enclosure with his milk. I went to the door, and found a girl, around thirteen, basically a kid still, swiping around every which way on her phone. "Hi, sorry I'm late. I just needed to get-" Ooops, I forgot to disguise myself. I did it in a haze to distract her. Maybe she'll second-guess herself now that I dressed a bit like her, but in male attire. She was wearing all-black with her pale face all smeared with makeup around the eyes and lips with black. I kind of liked that. But she did have some colorful frills on her skirt and had a streak of pink on her hair, which wasn't of my taste. "Yes?" I called, "I-I'm supposed to ssit, babysit for-" "Jasper? Oh. No need. I'm filling in for Raffy. You can go." She went away in a hurry.

It wasn't long until the mom, Kate, came back from her errand. She had two bags of random stuff, set it down on the sofa near the entrance, adjusted her new spectacles, and crashed on the adjacent seat. "It's so great that I can finally see you clearly Jas, I hope Raff wasn't too much trouble!" "No matter madam, he was as any human child is." For some reason, she glared at me after I spoke. "Your voice is incredibly deep! Have you thought of voice acting? I'm sure they'll hire goths like you even if you do look a little bit edgier than usual!" I wasn't sure what "voice acting" was, and what she meant by "edgy", as I was in slumber for quite a while, so I just replied "I'll look into it.", To which she interjected, "Wait, no, I don't want to wait another week for a babysitter! That stupid app service didn't even compensate for the delay. If I could even have you live here that would be perfect but it isn't in the options-" "That could be arranged. I am interested in in-house service, since I just came from h- uhh- *clears throat* abroad." Her eyes glistened. "Ohh, em, gee, REALLY?! That would be so perfect! You could use the guest room upstairs, and I'll just go prepare your new contract in a bit!"

"To tell you the truth, I was a bit worried when they showed me your track record in that app, having just 2 bookings last year. But when I found out that most rebooking comments are just because you dress this way, I took the risk. I really needed to get my new glasses and talk with the specialist without having the little dude around wreaking havoc in the store like last time! You really are a lifesaver!" Kate explained while I signed my sigil on the white piece of paper that just came out of a little machine that hummed the words flat on the sheet. I am now bound to the mortal. She may now command me as she pleases, although my contract only states that I am to look after the summoner child, not to allow visitors on days she is off, food allergies, and the only medicines I am allowed to administer in certain situations. It is refreshing to have a set of responsibilities not even remotely related to delivering harm to others, erasing memories, acquiring power, or performing some sort of kink. I kind of like this.

Human children are far more difficult to deal with than demon children. Demons are more wily and extremely manipulative, and you really need to stand your ground with them, and be cautious of your words. It's almost the same with humans, but I have to deal with much more excrement with these little larvae. The tears, sweat, puke, saliva, pee and poop along with occasional scrapes of blood caked in dirt are something that I needn't deal with back in the abyss nursery. Raffy's mom thinks I'm "heaven-sent", much to her naivety, but she doesn't know how grossed out I am. You know those old movies about possession, where the possessed vomit like an old water pump? Humans do that. The body tries its best to take out the demon but it can't, and it's just so disgusting. But what can you expect from someone made out of meat? Even Raffy's mom has had some vomiting spells and looked a bit paler recently. Her hair used to glow in the sunlight when she played with her son, and her cheeks used to be so rosy and warm-looking. That is not my doing, nor any influence of my demonic power. Her flesh vessel is just not keeping well.

I have tried to warn her of her illness, subtly at first, just mentioning that she doesn't look too well, she should get checked out, you know, the normal human way. She shrugged it off saying she's just tired, or she just didn't sleep well because blah, blah, blah... money issues, crappy government healthcare programs, whatever worldly excuse you can imagine. I usually wouldn't care about human mortality but this was my summoner's mother. I've had enough of her excuses. This had been going on for months! I finally confronted her one day and said, "If you don't take care of yourself, you're going to murder Raffy's mother. Go get yourself checked for his sake."

If I knew how to heal mortals, I would've done so with her. She was a bit different from the ones I've met before. She would respectfully listen to solicitors and evangelists going door to door before respectfully turning them down like a toddler being denied cookies before dinner. I admired her patience and gentle ruthlessness. She rarely ever had a fit of anger as she always considered the people and environment, and merely assumed the inferior circumstances, and/or brain capacity of the other party. She was very entertaining, and I'd hate for her to die young... but it wasn't looking good at all. I started asking around my arcane network about ways to heal her, but healing isn't particularly a specialty of our kind.

They did ask me why I was so invested in this human though, and I couldn't answer it well. I grew fond of her. That wasn't really a good enough reason for them to accept. I liked how she didn't want anything from me, be it power, fame, riches, or anything else. It still seems like a shallow reason. But ultimately, it was too late. Her flesh vessel was too corroded to function. Her time was inevitably coming, but I was also concerned for my summoner. What about him?

<p align="center">~~~</p>

"Rafael Pollock Dagonson! Please bring your parents tomorrow for a conference. Your vandalism has GOT to stop. This has been the fifth time!" Great, I've been caught… but no matter, the sigils are complete. Nobody will hound Mary anymore unless they'd want a pack of hellhounds at their butt as well. "Sorry Mrs. Tate, I'll paint over it, I promise! Please don't call mom!" It's a bit of a pain when your mom is a ghost, I don't particularly love the vessel she has to possess to be seen, it's just so embarrassing if they only knew! "No Raff, it's just been too many times. I need to talk to your parents. Give them this note, and I'll see them tomorrow afternoon. I will also call them later to confirm, so you won't get out of this!" Crap.

It's been thirteen years since mom met dad, and ten years since she passed. But dad is a demon and kind of negotiated for mom to stay a bit because of "their contract", but he actually just really loves mom. The thing is, he had to get a new vessel for her, and that's the big issue. She had to have a movable mouth to be able to speak, and the only dolls that would be viable for that, and look realistically human are the ones you get from kink shops. Now she possesses it whenever she has to deal with people, and I always feel awkward with her in that state. Dad's not an issue, he just needs to remember to keep his human form. I got startled by a hand that suddenly but stealthily brushed against mine, and passed me a little scrap of paper. I quickly put my hand in my pocket and walked home with my head hanging.

Along the way, I just dreaded having my demon dad and ghost, love-doll mom have that conference with my teacher, but Mary deserves the protection. She knows about my situation. Her mom saw dad before she was born, and told her how absolutely cool she thinks he is everyday since she was born two years later, and often lurked around. She has the same name as my dad, and said she was supposed to babysit me. Huh, small world.

About the Author

Mimie

Mimie is an INTP, Capricorn, Ox, Not Slytherin, who likes personality tests but forgets about them right after. She likes coffee, sweets, and has an unintentional collection of musical instruments.

www.ingramcontent.com/pod-product-compliance
Lightning Source LLC
LaVergne TN
LVHW041602070526
838199LV00046B/2104